First published in the UK in 2019
by New Frontier Publishing Europe Ltd.
Uncommon, 126 New King's Rd, Fulham, London SW6 4LZ
www.newfrontierpublishing.co.uk

ISBN: 978-1-912858-13-2

Edited by Stephanie Stahl
Designed by Verity Clark

Printed in China
10 9 8 7 6 5 4 3 2 1

The CAVEMAN Next Door

To Bry, Zach and Milo for all your love and support.
Also a big thank you to Team Plum for never giving up on Ogg and Penny.
Also to Wilma the dog for snoozing behind me while I made this book.

~ T T-D

The CAVEMAN Next Door

By Tom Tinn-Disbury

NEW FRONTIER PUBLISHING

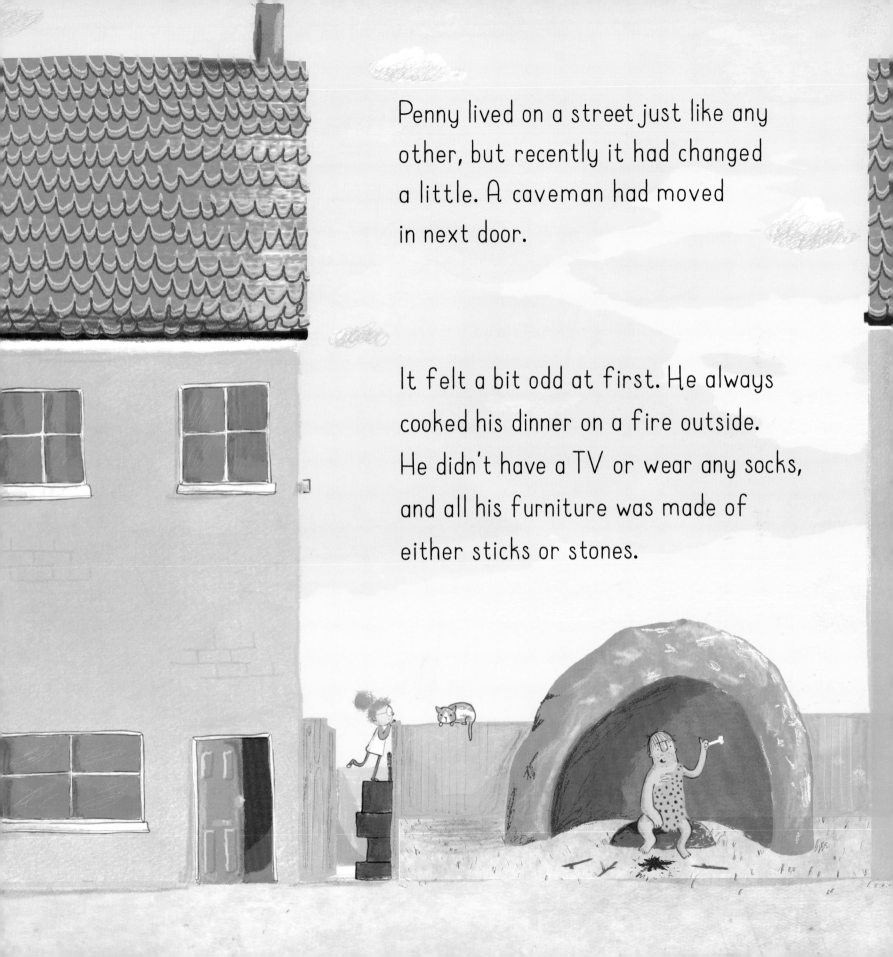

Penny lived on a street just like any other, but recently it had changed a little. A caveman had moved in next door.

It felt a bit odd at first. He always cooked his dinner on a fire outside. He didn't have a TV or wear any socks, and all his furniture was made of either sticks or stones.

All he would do is grunt.
It sounded like . . .

He often looked a little lost,
so one day after school, Penny
decided to show him around.

'Let's go to the library!' said Penny. It was her favourite place.
It seemed like a good start.
'Ogg-Ogg,' Ogg agreed.

'You can learn all sorts of things from books, such as new words,' said Penny. 'Like *Tyrannosaurus Rex*. Hmm maybe that's too difficult . . .

... what about Mackerel or Wizard? No, Ogg! We don't eat books, we read them!'

The librarian was very annoyed. She chased Penny and Ogg out of the library.

STOP EATING MY BOOKS!!

SORRY!!!

Ogg seemed upset. Penny thought a ride on the bus
might cheer him up. She always enjoyed
sitting on the top deck at the front.
'Oh no, Ogg! Get down!' cried Penny.
'We sit inside the bus!'

The bus driver was so cross that he refused to let them on the bus.

Ogg felt very sorry for getting it wrong again.
'Don't worry, Ogg,' said Penny. 'It's a lovely, sunny
day, let's take a walk through the park instead!'

Ogg loved being surrounded by nature and seeing all the different animals.
Penny tried to teach him some of their names but then ...

... Ogg spotted a fountain.

Ogg Drink!

'Ogg, no! That's not for drinking!' cried Penny.

The park ranger was very annoyed, and it took a lot of explaining from Penny to calm her down.

Ogg looked so sad that Penny thought a nice lunch might cheer him up, and it would be a good opportunity to teach him about table manners!

Ogg was trying his best, but his table manners weren't so good just yet. He ate the napkins, spilt his drink and put his arms in the tomato sauce. 'WhAt tHiS?' said Ogg, looking at the salt shaker. He then threw it over his shoulder with a shrug!

MmM, yuMMY FooD!

The waiter was furious,
he gave them the bill and
pointed to the door.

Poor Ogg, he didn't fit in at all.

'Don't worry, Ogg, we'll try again tomorrow,' said Penny.

'It's getting late. Let's go home.'

Ogg felt miserable and Penny really didn't know what to do.

Bright and early the next morning, Penny knocked on Ogg's cave.

As she walked in, she saw that the walls were covered with beautiful drawings of all of the adventures they had shared together.

'You are talented!'
said Penny.
'Tank you,' replied Ogg,
with a big smile.

Then Penny had an idea. Tomorrow was show and tell at school.
She could tell everyone about Ogg, and he might even learn
some new words!

The next day, Penny and Ogg arrived at school, feeling extremely excited.

'Today I have brought in my next door neighbour, Ogg. He's a caveman,' explained Penny.

'HaLLo, everyone,' said Ogg. 'MiCe to eeet yOu all!'

'Ogg is quite handy with a spear,

he can make furniture using almost any material . . .

... and he is really good at painting. Ogg, NO, not on the walls!'

Ogg was really upset to have caused such chaos at Penny's school. The children loved the classroom's new look though!

The head teacher wanted to see Ogg and Penny in his office.

Uh, oh, Penny thought.

'I found these interesting creations,' said the head teacher. 'Mister Ogg, would you like to stay a little longer and teach the children a thing or two about the natural world?'

'YeS. Ogg wOuLD LOVE TO!' exclaimed Ogg.
'We could even keep the pictures on the wall
for a bit,' suggested the head teacher.

'Well done, Ogg,' cheered Penny.

From that day onwards, Ogg became the new 'Natural World' teacher.

He showed eager children his caveman skills.

Everyone loved his lessons!

Ogg learned a lot from the children, too.

Morning Ogg!

And instead of the caveman next door,
he slowly became Ogg, the friend next door.

MoRNing Penny!

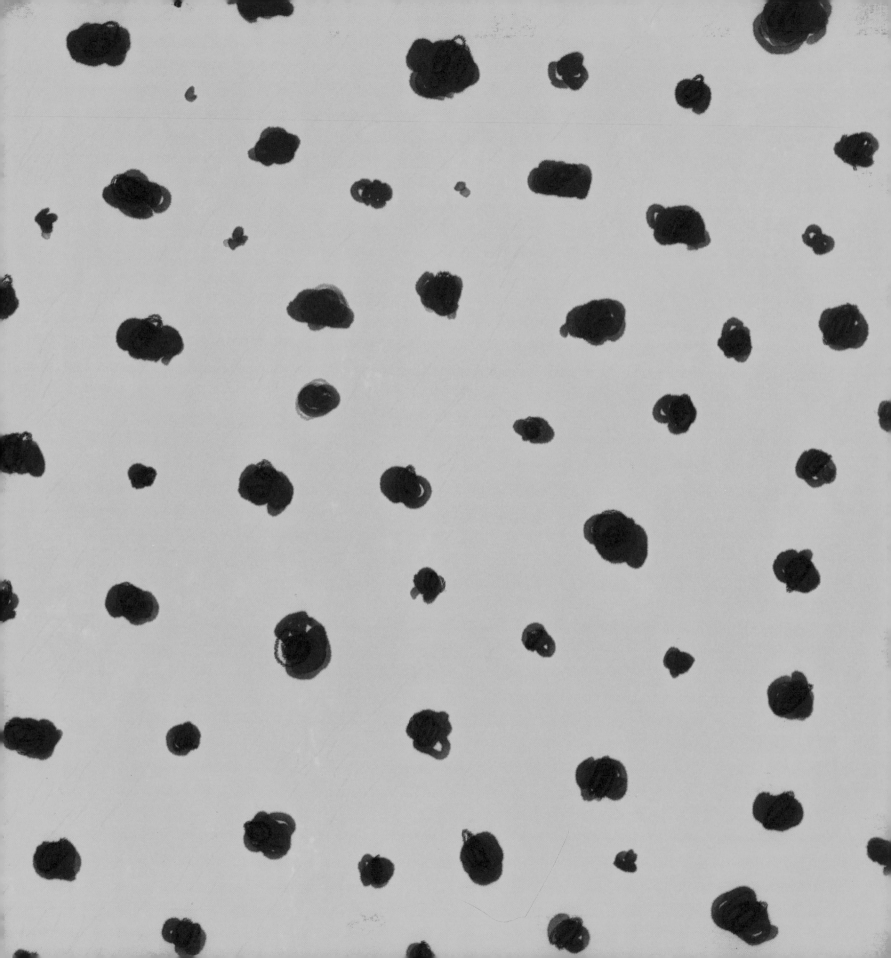